Butterbean's Café One Magical Night

Adapted by Christy Webster
Based on the teleplay "The Glowberry Fairy!" by Rosie DuPont
Illustrated by MJ Illustrations

A Random House PICTUREBACK® Book

Random House 🏠 New York

© 2020 Viacom International Inc. All rights reserved. Published in the United States by Random House Children's Books, a division of Penguin Random House LLC, 1745 Broadway, New York, NY 10019, and in Canada by Penguin Random House Canada Limited, Toronto. Pictureback, Random House, and the Random House colophon are registered trademarks of Penguin Random House LLC. Nickelodeon, Nick Jr., Butterbean's Café, and all related titles, logos, and characters are trademarks of Viacom International Inc.

rhcbooks.com

ISBN 978-0-593-12279-2

MANUFACTURED IN CHINA   10 9 8 7 6 5 4 3 2 1

Glow effect and production: Red Bird Publishing Ltd., U.K.

One summer afternoon, Cricket was reading about the legend of the Glowberry Fairy. Suddenly, someone shouted from the roof garden.

"Radical!" Jasper cried. "There are so many!"

"So many what?" Cricket asked as she flew up there.

"Raspberries," Jasper replied. "The first of the season."

Cricket and Jasper flew into the café.
"The first raspberries are ripe!" Cricket announced.
"Do you know what that means? The Glowberry Fairy
is coming tonight!"

Cricket read from her book. *"'When the first berries of the season are ripe, the Glowberry Fairy will fly through the night. Make her a berry-filled treat just so, and she'll make all the berries in the garden glow.'"*

Then she showed her friends a picture of the fairy.

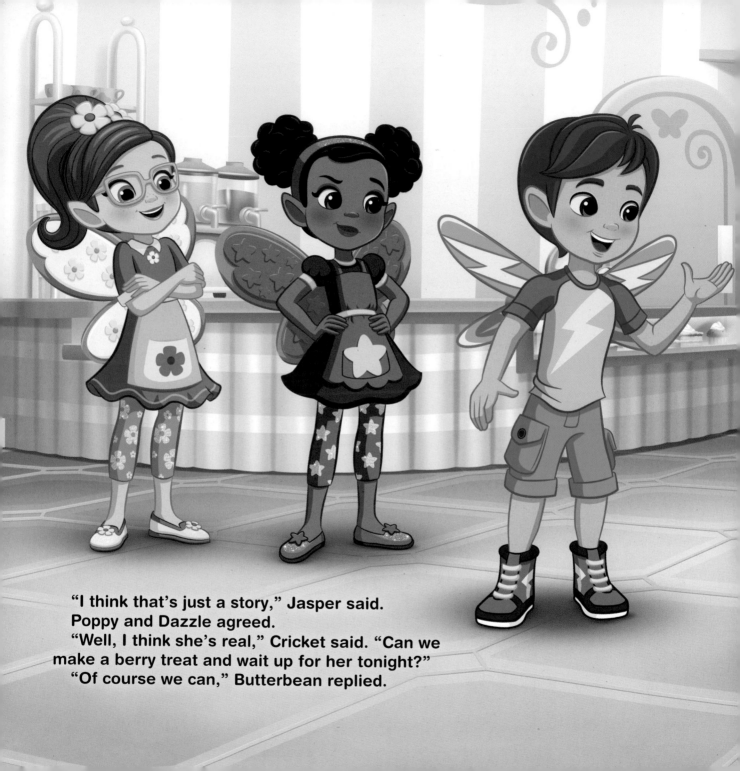

"I think that's just a story," Jasper said.
Poppy and Dazzle agreed.
"Well, I think she's real," Cricket said. "Can we make a berry treat and wait up for her tonight?"
"Of course we can," Butterbean replied.

Cricket set the table for the Glowberry Fairy, making it look just like one of the pictures in her book. She finished by leaving a raspberry muffin as a special treat for the fairy.

Then she started to wait.

"Cricket, she might not come if you're standing right next to the muffin all night," Butterbean said. That gave her an idea: they would go to the roof and watch for the Glowberry Fairy with a pair of binoculars.

Cricket still had a concern.
"What if we miss her?" she asked.
Butterbean pointed to the bell
above the door. "We just listen for
the jingle," she said.

The sisters kept watching. Cricket couldn't see anything!
But then she spotted a little light dancing near the house
next door.

"I think I see her!" Cricket cried.

"Where?" Butterbean asked.

Cricket looked through her binoculars and saw . . .

. . . their neighbor taking out the trash.
Cricket sighed. "It's just Mr. Hops's flashlight,"
she said.

"I know the rest of the team doesn't believe in the Glowberry Fairy," Cricket said, "but do you?"

"I do believe there's magic all around us, so you never know," Butterbean replied, but she didn't sound convinced.

Just then, Cricket heard a jingling sound.

The sisters gasped. "The door!" they said at the same time.

Cricket and Butterbean snuck downstairs to try to catch a glimpse of the Glowberry Fairy. And they saw . . .

. . . Poppy and Dazzle! They were setting out treats for the Glowberry Fairy, too.

"We don't know if she's real or a story," Poppy said.

"But if she's real, we want to see her," Dazzle explained.

Then they heard a thump! It came from the kitchen. They all hurried in to see the fairy.

It was Jasper. He was leaving out a
raspberry treat, too!

"What are you doing here?" Cricket asked.

"If the Glowberry Fairy is going to make the
garden glow, I've got to see it!" he said.

Now the whole Bean Team was watching for the Glowberry Fairy. After a while, Cricket spotted a flickering light near Ms. Marmalady's café.

"There!" she cried.

Everyone looked.

"I see her!" Butterbean said.

"Oh my squash!" Dazzle said.

The light stopped flickering, and the
friends could hear Spork and Spatch arguing.
"I want to turn off the light!" Spork said.
"No, *I* want to!" Spatch replied.
The Bean Team laughed. Spork and Spatch
were definitely not the Glowberry Fairy!
They heard the front door jingle again.
They hurried down into the café . . .

. . . and turned on a light. It was Cookie! She had her paw in the treat jar.

There was no sign of the Glowberry Fairy.

"It's almost morning," Dazzle said.

"I guess it is just a story," Jasper said.

"We should get some rest," said Butterbean.

Cricket didn't want to give up. "Can I leave my muffin out?" she asked. "Just in case?"

"Of course, Cricket," Butterbean said, and the team headed home.

As Cricket slowly fluttered across the bridge a little behind the others, she heard the jingle of the door back at the café. She turned and saw something quickly fly by. Could it be . . . the Glowberry Fairy?

She flew as fast as she could, calling for the others to follow.

After Cricket burst into the café, she saw that someone had eaten part of her raspberry muffin!
She hurried up the stairs.

Outside, Cricket saw something darting
through the air. It was the Glowberry Fairy!

"*Now* do you believe in the Glowberry
Fairy, Butterbean?" Cricket asked.
"I sure do," Butterbean said.
"Thanks to you."